For Christophe, the most "triple-L" of the world—MS

For Suzanne, Joke, Ingrid buuv, and Connie—GvdL

Copyright © 2006 by Lemniscaat b.v. Rotterdam
Originally published in the Netherlands under the title *Het Monsterlied* by Lemniscaat b.v. Rotterdam
All rights reserved—CIP data is available
Printed and bound in Belgium
First U.S. edition

FRONT STREET
An Imprint of Boyds Mills Press, Inc.
A Highlights Company

815 Church Street
Honesdale, Pennsylvania 18431

MONSTERSONG

Mathilde Stein **&** Gerdien van der Linden

FRONT STREET & LEMNISCAAT

I'm lying in bed, but I can't get to sleep.
I've tried counting sheep to a thousand and three.
It doesn't work right. You want to know why?
A monster is pestering me.

He's under my bed. I can hear him down there.
He giggles and growls and sings a strange song.
He's coming to get me! And I want to know
what's keeping Mommy so long.

She's finally here, but she just starts to laugh
when I tell her what's scaring me so.
"Here in your room? Well, I'll just take a peek."
She checks all around, she looks high and low.

"Yes, there are five here. Five exceptional cuties!
Come here, little fellow,"
she says with a smile,
as she pulls a scary one out from below.

The monster is green and he looks really nasty.
He rolls his eyes as I stare in alarm.
But Mom says, "How nice of you to visit,"
and she cuddles him in her arm.

I shiver and shake. I can hardly believe it.
"Watch out for those teeth, Mom. One bite and you're dead!"
"Don't be silly, my boy. Now move over, will you?
There's plenty of room in your bed."

She's got to be kidding. A monster beside me?
Right under the blankets, to sleep here all night?
"Pretty cozy, huh?" Mom asks. "It will be even cozier
when the other four monsters get tucked in tight."

Monster Two's nose is dripping.
His nails are grimy, broken, and black.
"Wash up," Mom tells him.
I hope once he's done that he doesn't come back.

While Monster Two scrubs his toes,
Monster One pinches my arm.
"He's teasing me, Mom, and I can't make him stop it."
"Don't tattle now, darling. He'll do you no harm.

"These monsters have rules that are different.
Perhaps you're not used to the games that they play.
But don't start in crying. That won't solve a thing.
Try being more friendly. Now, what do you say?"

I don't say a word, but I move over further
and fearfully wait for the next one to show.
Then Monster Two takes one great leap,
and lands on my tummy and hollers, "Hello!"

Mom kneels down and looks under the bed.
"Now, let's see, who's next to come out and play?
Are you Number Three? Come on, then, don't dawdle."
"No, Mom! If you leave him, he might go away.

"Don't you see him down there with his cruel little eyes?
Just look at those fangs! How they shimmer and shine!"
Mom says, "My dear, we are all so different.
That's what makes the world so incredibly fine."

She gives him pajamas and puts him in bed.
Now it's so crowded I can't wriggle or roll,
but I do see that this new bedmate of mine
looks dangerously like a troll.

Number Four props himself on the side of the bed.
That's when it becomes painfully clear
from the odor that fills the room:
this fellow has not had a bath in more than a year.

On his warty old head is a tangle of knots
infested with bugs who are waving at me!
Mom says, "Hand me a comb, dear. I'll do what I can
to clean up this fellow and make him lice-free."

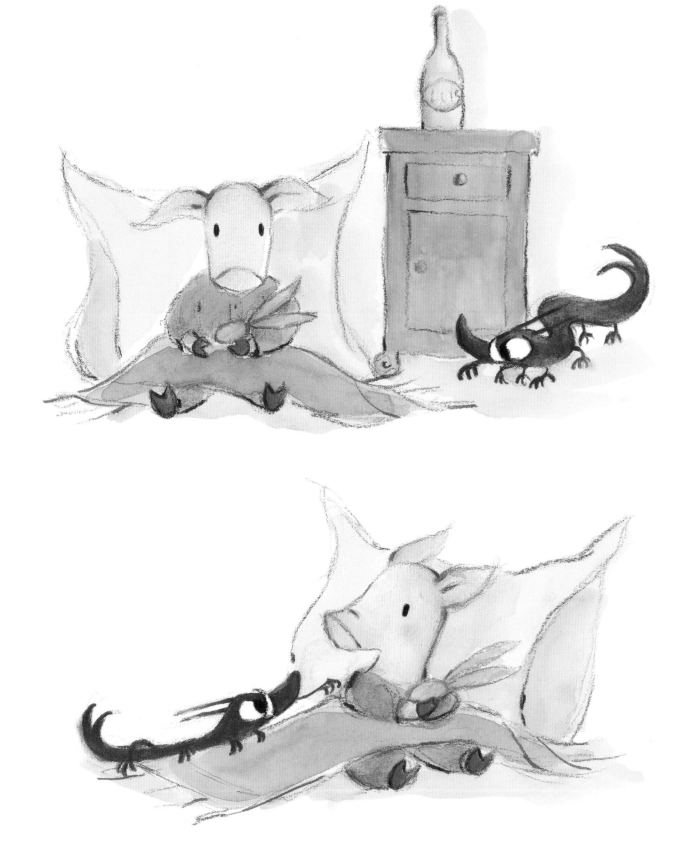

Here comes Monster Number Five.
He glares at me with one big fierce eye.
He's got eight little legs and one giant claw.
He creeps under my blanket—he's quick and he's sly.

Mommy laughs. "He likes you. How sweet."
He pulls on my hair and gives me a poke.
"He just wants to play. Why don't you join him?"
But I don't like his games, and I don't get the joke.

She puts him in bed and he's sitting right here.
The monsters are growling and kicking about.
"How nice," Mommy says. "You've so many new friends.
Now you won't be alone when the lights are all out.

"You can go back to sleep. We've solved the whole problem.
Not one single monster left under your bed.
So close your eyes tight and drift into dreams.
Believe me, they're gone—it's just as I said."

Monster One hisses softly,
"Hey guys, let's raise a ruckus, what do you say?"
"Please, Mommy, don't leave me. I don't want to stay."
"Lights out," Mom says, and she tiptoes away.

Then the monsters start chuckling.
They slink up beside me, they shriek, and they groan.
I can't breathe a breath, and I can't move a muscle.
How can I get them to leave me alone?

"Uh, Monsters," I ask a little bit slyly,
"do you feel as crowded as me?
My mom's got a bed as big as the ocean.
It's just down the hall. Go look and you'll see."

The monsters are gone in the blink of an eye. Amazing!
Now I'll be able to sleep through the night.
And won't Mom be glad to find five new friends
in her bed when she turns out the light?